George Lunt

The Rhymers' Club

SALZWASSER
VERLAG

George Lunt

The Rhymers' Club

Reprint of the original, first published in 1859.

1st Edition 2022 | ISBN: 978-3-37513-370-2

Verlag (Publisher): Salzwasser Verlag GmbH, Zeilweg 44, 60439 Frankfurt, Deutschland
Vertretungsberechtigt (Authorized to represent): E. Roepke, Zeilweg 44, 60439 Frankfurt, Deutschland
Druck (Print): Books on Demand GmbH, In de Tarpen 42, 22848 Norderstedt, Deutschland

THE

𝕽𝖍𝖞𝖒𝖊𝖗𝖘' 𝕮𝖑𝖚𝖇,

By

AN HONORARY MEMBER.

Misce stultitiam consiliis brevem;
Dulce est desipere in loco.—*Horace.*

New York:
1859.

THE RHYMERS' CLUB.

I.

Ten thousand gas-lights gleam'd a placid white
Athwart the city's sleep-composing face,
Speckling the blackness of a moonless night
And guiding each belated homeward pace;
Nor tavern, theatre nor public place
The loiterer longer tempted to its bowers;
And Sound had yielded for the wonted space
To Silence, with its ever shifting powers,
Th' alternate sceptre over the revolving hours.

II.

Within a cloud-capt garret, seated round
A penny-a-liner's hospitable board,
Of hungry wits and thirsty midnight found
A company whose mirth and wassail roar'd,
As oysters were dipp'd and ale was pour'd,
Gay spirits glorying in a seedy lot
And the scant dainties chance might them afford;
Boasting of lineage short and knowing not
Nor known to that we call society, I wot.

III.

Their locks wore every curious length,
Their beards of studied quaintness each degree,
And threadbare coats contrasted with the strength
And thoroughness of their hilarity;
'Twas droll the sparkle of their eyne to see,
Of past or future keen forgetfulness,
And satisfaction running o'er their glee;
Despite the signs which blabb'd the sordid stress
Of those mean cares that cling where'er they once
    possess.

IV.

To want of Luxury life-long inured
And saddest dearth of dear, domestic bliss,
They such privation carelessly endured,
Nor griev'd for what they ne'er had learn'd to miss;
Each deem'd a tolerable state were his,
Or peradventure dream'd of a career
Wherein his brighten'd destiny should kiss
Consenting Fortune, and loud Fame's breath clear
Trumpet his name upon the world's astonished ear.

V.

Hard was the soil whereon their life was sown,
Exposed to airs with evil influence fraught
And all by weeds of indigence o'ergrown.
Their good if care parental e'er besought
Or friendly nurture shap'd their earliest thought,
Too soon they lost th'incalculable boon;
No costly schools their growing culture taught;
Driv'n prematurely on the world alone,
Their faults their Fates imposed, their merits were their
   own.

VI.

Yet not unlearn'd they manhood's threshold cross'd,
Nor held in Ignorance's rule unkind;
Their native strength aside her fetters toss'd
That aye the unresisting rabble bind:
For irrepressible is the strong mind
And will its own emancipation seize;
And they at stall and library did find
The subtle food which can forever please
The soul's keen appetite, though it may ne'er appease.

VII.

And now Imagination's wings they plume,
To seek the Muses' high abode aspire,
And on the flight the daring thought presume
To pluck from Heav'n some portion of that fire
Which warms to moving melody the lyre.
Not groves nor pastures, meadows, brooks nor all
The treasures of the rural earth inspire
Their lays, but man and what affairs we call,
And scenes and deeds that hap within the city's wall.

VIII.

The penny-a-liner was of middle age,
A Fortune-spurn'd and Fortune-spurning wight;
A solemn front he wore and aspect sage
And Solomon by his companions hight,
Though named not so in the baptismal rite;
Nor needs it that the Muse's history
His nomen or cognomen should recite,
Or whether any genealogic tree
Or regular and lawful christening had he.

IX.

Enough that, howe'er born or howe'er bred,
And whether tenderly or roughly cradled,
His years full long in penury had sped;
Of needs with a sore burden was he saddled;
O'er seas of debt his life's poor skiff he paddled,
More full of perils for their shallowness;
Troubles that had a weaker spirit addled;
More pinching from their very narrowness;
For petty ills than larger sorrows chafe not less.

X.

But little did he mind the shafts of care
That hover'd alway pointing at his breast,
And seem'd man's common weakness not to share;
Nor power of dread condition he confess'd,
By chance elated ne'er and ne'er depress'd,
But view'd the world with fine serenity
Wherein he did high as his attic rest,
Sooth'd the complaining hours with Poesy
And lofty temper held of high Philosophy.

XI.

Yet not because his soul, so fortified,
Was proof against the vulgar woes of Time
Did he reject what joys his lot supplied;
Nor his was that austerity sublime
Which buys exemption from life's suff'rings prime
With sourly disregarding each prime good;
He took what pleasures Fate vouchsafed to him;
And jovial ever was his inner mood,
Crusted with gravity his guests well understood.

XII.

Soon as the fierceness of the feast was done,
A murmur all the circle did pervade,
Demanding the new song of Solomon,
His muse's latest born; nor he gainsay'd,
Nor any coy and needless lingering made;
Complying as beseem'd so wise a man;
No preface spake, no critic's mercy pray'd;
But straight the pleas'd rehearsal he began
And thus the lately ruralizing numbers ran.

New York:

A SATIRE.

Though now escap'd, for all the fervid year,
From town and tumult to my acres dear
Whose shades the Hudson's busy waters view,
The restless muse will winter themes pursue.
What varied landscape or what fertile field
Can e'er such products or such fancies yield
As hold the mind and every sense beguile
At yonder river-wash'd and flinty isle?

Whose central heat attracts all enterprise
And radiates the globe with merchandise,
A heart whose pulses throb to either pole,
Vortex of all the passions of the soul !
There crowd life's aspects with obstrep'rous pains
And lurid Contrast o'er each aspect reigns ;
There Poverty's thick-peopled sheds arise
Close where the roofs of Affluence split the skies ;
There jostle sage and fool in daily round ;
There Truth and Fraud career on mutual ground ;
There brushes Virtue's hem the hem of Vice ;
There dunce and genius each his mission plies ;
There all extremes at once compel the sight
And each condition there confronts its opposite.

The busy fleets that oft all oceans stud
There rest by squalid wharves of rotting wood,
While public millions yearly melt away
On useless works, of public thieves the prey.
Yet charity hath builded well and wide
Her fair foundations there on every side ;
Religion's temples thickly point on high
With admirable unanimity ;
And Justice within stately walls maintains
The melancholy hosts her doom restrains,
But for herself fantastic worship finds
Perform'd around dilapidated shrines ;

Clear Science unctuous with endowment smiles
And pompous Commerce raises costly piles ;
While private wealth its careless thousands flings
On democratic dwellings fit for kings.

Metropolis of Liberty's land vast !
Haven of fierce republicans and fast !
Full oft, what thy peculiar glory blights,
Thy citizens accept their equal rights
And common freedom in, alas ! the sense
Of vanity and fashion and pretence.
The newly rich whom vulgar arts of trade
Have robb'd of one, nor giv'n another grade,
Poor wanderers along the social scale,
Rest for whose feet to find all efforts fail ;
Endow'd with narrow gifts in gain t'employ ;
Denied the grace or sense that gain t'enjoy ;
Unsatisfied, unquiet, vacant, drear,
To follies strange devote the livelong year.
Their wealth a boast, their homes a vain parade
Of tawdry splendors anxiously display'd,
In heartless waste they entertainment hold,
And hospitality in riot cold ;
Trifles their care ; laborious their ease ;
Saddens their mirth, their pleasures fail to please ;
Their souls' best worship do they give alone
To Etiquette as to a god unknown ;

In friendship and in love they sink the heart;
Exist in artifice devoid of art;
Contrive all gifts and senses to abuse
And life's each good ingeniously misuse.
They storm the gazing wonder of the throng,
As borne in tinsell'd equipage along,
While perch'd aloft in melancholy pairs,
Wearing stiff liveries and monstrous airs,
Bedizen'd, new-fledg'd flunkies tortur'd ride;
Some born the prancing steeds' career to guide,
Some doom'd to dance their service out before
The glistening chariot's ever-swinging door,
Whose panels fiercely glow, as limn'd in fire,
With rampant lions or with griffons dire,
Heraldic blazon of some warrior's name
That, with th' invading Norman, conq'ring came.
Their lineage but a generation trace,
Some sainted tailor heads the haughty race,
Or haply from a cooper's loins they spring
In lately budded pride now blossoming,
Or once a cobbler's still preserv'd by fate
Their patriarch, mindless of his former state.
Thus, all unspher.ed, through life they conscious go,
Aiming at what they ne'er exactly know.
The town in keen derision holds its sides,
Envies and imitates and still derides.

Alas! that emulation such should lure
From Honor's peaceful walk th'ambitious poor
To paths where Crime decoys their footsteps blind
And lurking Ruin grimly steals behind.

How few of all that gather on th' exchange,
And give to traffic · energy's chief range,
Keep nature sound nor sacrifice what part
Best fills the head or occupies the heart!
One scheme's two paltry halves divide their care,
To buy cheap one, the other to sell dear;
Till growing greed creeps o'er the yielding soul,
Subdues each portion and absorbs the whole.
See where the pet of Fortune takes his way!
Adown at morn, at evening up Broadway;
Aspiring men his salutations claim,
Proud enterprises crave his potent name,
His brows financial joy or woe diffuse,
And ev'n the needy state his favor sues.
By what exclusive thoughts is he possess'd?
What high resolves expand the great man's breast?
To him Philosophy no light hath shown,
Science vouchsafed arithmetic alone,
And life-long strangers to his brain and heart
The charm of letters, the delights of art.
His youth's fair aims untimely mammon-bent,
His manhood's purpose is net ten per cent.;

His waning life no loftier joys shall know
Than from accumulating dollars flow;
No visions his dissolving moments cheer
Save dreams of buying cheap and selling dear;
And death will quench his occupation, when
May peace be with his peddling soul!   Amen!

A lot more drear and harsher fate attend
The wretch who seeks in vain the self-same end;
Him the capricious goddess seems to sue,
Spreading her baubles in his constant view;
Eager he runs and thinks the whole to clasp,
She pulls the playthings just beyond his grasp;
Impetuous he the foil'd attempt renews
And gains unnatural fire as he pursues;
Pleas'd at his torture, the divine coquette
Recedes and nicely balks his labor yet;
Both persevere till impotence and age
His ardor kill, subdue his trembling rage,
Defeat and vain pursuit at once cut short
And end the disappointment and the sport.
Behind he looks and lo! a dismal waste
Of crime and folly not to be retraced;
Long cover'd but concealable not long;
He groans and quivers in a weakness strong
And quits the world by a self-murd'ring hand,
Or skulks, like Schuyler, on some foreign strand

Shunning each known and every honest gaze,
Companionless to drag the remnant of his days.

For gold or power, for pleasure or repute,
Fierce multitudes each public place dispute
And turn life's labors to confusion bad,
A scramble multifarious and mad.
As when a caldron, over flames dispos'd,
Boils, filled with liquids variously compos'd,
While dregs descend, the scum is mounting seen,
Leaving all purity conceal'd between ;
So from low alleys and from dirty lanes
Office a swarming host of statesmen gains,
And Conscript Fathers who on council floors
Appear like rats rang'd round a granary's stores :
Sometime a scoundrel, with demurest air,
May sit in the chief magistrate's high chair,
A man who, to secure his meanest end,
The city's latest drop of blood would spend ;
The boldest quack the highest favor gains
And o'er the populace sheer humbug reigns ;
While ev'n some selfish priests will reach renown
Among the worldly wonders of the town,
If with their fame the public ear be cramm'd,
Indiff'rent whether flocks be sav'd or damn'd.

That citizen is blest who bears his soul,
With wakeful, easy, and serene control,
Above the motives which the vulgar guide,
False pleasure, false ambition and false pride ;
Who, having honest cares, confronts their pow'r
And, seeking competence, sighs for no more ;
Who passing things with human int'rest minds
And every homely happiness refines ;
Who can a play enjoy with vision clean
And scent no needless sin behind the scene ;
Who with taught judgment, and with relish pure,
Ranges the realms of art and literature ;
Who walks alike apart, in conscience brac'd,
From levity or cant, meanness or waste ;
Unspotted by that complaisance which draws
The rabble's noisy censure or applause.

I wish to mingle in the city's throng
Enough to know its right side and its wrong ;
To see its works, its spirit to discern,
Look its disguises through, its follies learn :
So that I may not, like th' untravel'd boor,
Gap foolish wonder at its splendors poor,
Nor, like the crooked cynic, falsely wise,
Its fashions, pleasures, comforts all despise ;
Not to its sordid schemes addict my life,
Nor yet completely shun its active strife ;

But of its good enough industrious gain,
Heedful avoid its ill, and best maintain,
While moving with the motion of mankind,
The true and steadfast balance of the mind.

XIII.

So died the strain away whose stately flow
No whisper rude nor sound impertinent
Presum'd disturb, or seem in aught to show
A suff'ring audience's discontent;
But revelry was hush'd and converse pent,
As if they did on admiration sup,
Till, when the last note gave their voices vent,
The ale's impatient foam crown'd every cup,
And all the rhymers round the festal board stood up.

XIV.

No silly phrase of lying flattery
Was now the silent poet's flat reward,
No poignant sting of envious irony,
From hostile critic or from rival bard,
The pride with which he wore his laurels marr'd.
Their partial view pass'd all but merit o'er ;
Unstudied praise was their sincere award,
And three times three loud cheers and one cheer more
That peradventure sleeping neighbors startled sore.

XV.

Enthusiasm and drink subsiding slow,
Vocif'rous honors caught another name,
Ezekiel, second of the rhyming row,
The son of love and of a Thespian dame
From whom he took naught but a borrow'd name ;
For, though she once with art and mimic fire
The comic stage triumphant trod to fame,
Yet, when she did in penury expire,
Left him to guess of all mankind who was his sire.

XVI.

Thus was he cast with those behind the scenes,
From all the earnest of his race apart,
Cut off from action's every other means
And held, though all unfitted for the part,
Unwilling devotee to irksome art.
Of mediocrity the sense and dread
His spirit rode and wore his rugged heart;
While years came o'er him with a creeping tread
And sprinkled silver o'er his melancholy head.

XVII.

His form was mighty and his sturdy brow
Majestical o'erhung a visage vast,
That sluggish now would seem and lively now,
Changing as o'er his ponderous features pass'd
Gleams from his active soul electric cast;
Heavy his eye but of a vision keen
For fact though hid in thick disguises fast;
Perhaps by peering in its deep serene
Might slumb'ring fires of sensibility be seen.

XVIII.

A strong, square-trotting Pegasus he strode,
That caper'd solemnly on solid ground,
Not form'd for prancing an ethereal road,
Nor train'd to tread the soft cerulean round
Or, fancy-spurr'd, among the stars to bound :
On whose broad back secure he sat upright
And sang plain truth though homely it might sound :
Nor let the timid moralist take fright
While the rough melody I faithfully recite.

XIX.

Ah ! little deem the gentle, high-behaved,
Proud priest and pharisee self-satisfied
What stalwart souls well worthy to be saved,
The fearful pale of sympathy outside,
Stand peering through in sadness or in pride ;
Or, stung by sense of cold exclusion long,
And slinking in abash'd resentment hide,
Who, if once beckon'd from the verge of wrong,
Of righteousness would be glad champions and strong.

The Offertory:

A SUNDAY LYRIC.

I.

Upon a holy Sabbath morn I sat,
  Amongst a multifarious congregation,
Beneath the vault of a high temple that
  Was Worship's by most solemn consecration,
Whither were wont poor souls in numbers great
  Betake themselves for weekly consolation,
Such as is either gain'd from real devotion
Or springs from some quite different emotion.

II.

The chimes roll'd out their latest, loit'ring sound ;
  Its first and faintest up the organ took ;
This slowly grew into a swell profound
  Which all the air and solid fabric shook
And spread Solemnity's grave mantle round ;
  All knees were bent, devout was every look ;
The litany and service then were read,
The prayers utter'd and responses said.

III.

The minister and people seem'd to be
   For once unmindful of all worldly wishes,
In heavenly contemplation wrapt, and free
   From cares of earth or of its loaves or fishes,
Its pow'r or pomp, its fame or vanity,
   Or any joy that sinful souls ravishes ;
When, lo ! there shock'd the ear what sound d'ye think ?
A sharp, metallic, oft-repeated clink.

IV.

Obtrusive sound ! that suddenly did bring
   The heaven-lifted spirit back to earth,
As with hard censure of her wandering
   From things of solid, measurable worth ;
And hint severe where thought might safely cling ;
   Apart from dreams of unsubstantial birth ;
And the assembly ready seem'd to drink
That hint and lesson from the noisy clink.

V.

The priest read loudly, " Let your light so shine
   Before men that—" the rest of the hortation
Was lost upon a dame in raiment fine,
   Gay priestess of the flaunting rites of Fashion,

Who rustled ostentatiously benign,
   And drew the eyes of all the congregation,
Before she parted with the piece of gold
Which of her piety and riches told.

VI.

" Lay not up treasures for yourselves on earth,"
   Was by a needy clerk interpreted,
Stirring alike thereby contempt and mirth,
   As if the lesson solemnly had read
" Give the sole dollar from thy purse's dearth ;
   Ev'n though thou ow'st it for thy coat or bread."
And the poor creature, yielding, freely gave
That which his creditors of right should have.

VII.

Again ; " He that hath pity on the poor
   Lendeth unto the Lord." An ancient man,
Of tottering form infirm and locks all hoar,
   Who had outlived life's ordinary span,
Harden'd in making much, or little, more ;
   Till wealth did end what poverty began,
Consider'd well what us'ry he might win ;
Then dropp'd a pinch'd, reluctant shilling in.

VIII.

" Whate'er ye would that men should do to you,
    Ev'n so do unto them," said with grave stress,
Was message vain to one whose visage blue
    Was pucker'd with pretended holiness,
With feignèd goodness penetrated through,
    As if he blandly all the world would bless:
It was the wily, formal hypocrite,
And the bank note he gave was counterfeit.

IX.

A woman sober as the weeds she wore,
    Oppress'd by Poverty, by Labor worn
And mark'd with wrinkling Grief's dread ravage sore,
    A faded remnant of a life forlorn,
Provoking thus in her observers or
    Reflecting pity or unthinking scorn,
Cast in the plate its best-deserving prize,
Severely hoarded for the sacrifice.

X.

A little, lisping, curl'd and laughing child,
    Too young the meaning of its act to know,
A fresh and tender soul not yet defiled,
    As soon it must be, if it stay below,

With fair, unconscious eagerness, beguiled
   Its parent of a penny to bestow.
Heav'n must have smiled, disarm'd of all offence,
To see the offering of Innocence.

XI.

So all the worshipers, with one accord,—
   Mov'd by a thousand undetermin'd shades
Of vanity or fear, hope of reward,
   Love, duty, all that hinders sin or aids,
Motives approv'd of heav'n or heav'n-abhorr'd,
   What elevates the soul and what degrades,—
Together pour'd their motley contribution,
All for the Church's use or distribution.

XII.

The last deposit's final, clinking sound
   Was with a cadence of the organ blended ;
The deacons, who had borne the basin round,
   Unto the chancel reverently wended ;
The priest reliev'd them with an air profound
   And the most interesting rite was ended,
When all the offerings rattlingly were mingled,
And even on the very altar jingled.

XX.

Perhaps some weariness began to fill
The rhymers ere the second lay was done;
For aye of solid things a surfeit will
Come when we scarcely deem the feast begun;
And pleasure veereth as the moments run.
But sign of flagging heed you might not see,
And high decorum held their eyes upon
The heavy bard, though wish'd they inwardly
The lighter harp of David, poet number three.

XXI.

A peasant's birth and peasant's childhood his,
Obscure, he long'd to shun a peasant's fate,
Far find the height where Learning's glory is
And gain the entrance at Art's temple's gate.
No purpose had his toil, his soul no mate,
While listlessly he turn'd his native sod,
And palely brooded on his low estate,
Till finally he fled the loathèd clod,
And, weary, scared and lone, the city's pavement trod.

XXII.

His pencil,—rude, original, untaught,—
To catch the landscape's momentary phase,
And hold the clouds on canvas, oft had sought,
But ne'er till then, in rapture and amaze,
Did he on Art's acknowledg'd glories gaze.
Year after year he dream'd and strove till he
Beheld fulfill'd a dream of early days,
His pictures in the annual gallery,
Though hung so high that venal critics could not see.

XXIII.

So still in sad neglect he play'd his part,
And cheerful worship'd where his soul adored;
Still wrought some useful drudgeries of art,
To pay for frugal shelter, bed and board;
And still on wings of hope and fancy soar'd,
His lot was single, and no mistress his
To charm the leisure that his strength restored,
Except a muse of lively qualities,
And gaily she produced, for our occasion, this.

The Chambermaid.

A ROMANCE.

On the broad staircase of the great hotel,
By the first grave daylight there that fell,
The early traveler, scarce awake,
Bustling his hurried leave to take,
A figure did pass, whose image fair
Thence journeyed with him everywhere.

An ample pitcher in her hand she bare,
As lightly she tripp'd along the broad stair,
And she meekly glanc'd at the going guest,
Which carried a trouble unto his breast;
For he was doom'd thenceforth to bear
The haunting remembrance everywhere.

It is the form of Isabel,
The fairest maid of the great hotel.
Oh! she is soft! oh! she is fair!
Her eyes are blue,—brown is her hair;
Slender is she, and debonair;
And her image goes with him everywhere.

The young and haughty lord is he
Of acres broad in the west countree;
But what are acres now to him
Who hath a sleeping and waking dream,
A teasing vision of pleasing care,
By night and by day and everywhere!

Why sticks the burden to his soul
And from his being will not roll,
Filling him with disquietude
Of passion wild and woful mood?
Ah! to rid himself he doth not care,
But cherisheth it everywhere.

Lost are the joys he knew before,
Nor willeth he old pleasures more;
His lands and treasures spurnèd are
And give place in his heart to the new-found care;
Upon land and sea he journeyeth far,
And that image is with him everywhere.

At last he returneth, fain to rest,
To the great hotel a wearied guest,
Whence he took the burden that him opprest;
And he meeteth again, on the same broad stair,
At midnight, by the gas's glare,
Her whose image was with him everywhere.

" Maiden, thy name and story tell.".
" Oh, yes : my name is Isabel;
My sire he was a Celtic knight,
And Sir Shillelah was he hight ;
Gentle and rich and great was he,
In the greenest land beyond the sea,
With a castle high and a manor wide,
And I was his darling and his pride.
A noble lady was my mother ;
I had no sister and no brother;
Our life was the highest bliss below ;
'T was well my parents should not know
What dreary fortunes since befel
Their orphan child, their Isabel !
I had a shaggy pony, he
Would draw or carry none but me ;
And many a furr'd or feather'd pet,
I fondle them in mem'ry—yet—

" My tale is long; I'll make it brief:
And now I come to my great grief.
One day my father and mother died,
And I saw them buried side by side ;
And I was left their only heir,
Without a soul to help me bear
The fearful load of my despair.

" They thought to leave me, when they died,
The castle high and manor wide;
But it chanc'd that I inherited
A tedious suit at law instead;
And another, alas! in chancery;
So I was driven bye and bye
From the manor wide and the castle high.
Then I wander'd forth on the king's highway,
And felt like a foolish sheep astray:
I carried my clothes and jewels tied
In a weighty parcel at my side;
But it soon grew light, for every day
I gave some jewel or thing to pay
My entertainers on the way.

" 'T was a fearful road I journey'd o'er,
For me who had journey'd ne'er before,
But in a stately coach and four.
For days and weeks I wander'd on,
E'er growing weary, worn and wan,
Till I did move like one infirm.
But every labor hath its term;
And I, at last, came where the sea
Spreads out in its immensity
And soothes with murmurs mild the shore,
Or frights with a tumultuous roar.

A ship with all sails set was there,
And she was named The Bridgetine,
And eager look'd to skim the brine ;
And loud the burly master sware,—
From both eyes brushing sudden tears,
When I had told my woes, my fears,—
If I would take a passage free
And his ship's hospitality,
He'd place me on a kinder shore
Where Fortune had perchance in store,
Among the equal and the free,
Some happier moments ev'n for me.

" I thank'd him from a swelling heart ;
For I had nought from which to part,
But my native land, which I bade adieu !
And we glided forth on the waters blue.
For forty days and nights we sped,
Without a threat'ning cloud o'erhead
Or angry wave beneath our feet ;
Another sail we did not meet,
Nor once see land in peering round
The blue horizon's circling bound ;
But a fair breeze and pathway clear
Slow brought us to this hemisphere ;

And one bright morn we landed by
A place they call the battery.
From the ship I came to the great hotel ;
I try to serve its master well,
And to do my new-learnt duty try,
Maid of the chambers, Isabel."

The pretty tale he doubteth not ;
He offereth her his home, his lot ;
And the haughty lady now is she
Of those acres broad in the west countree :
All that lord's riches she doth share,
And goeth with him everywhere.

XXIV.

Till David's harp its closing note did sound,
The Rhymers heard in silence and delight ;
But then their last reserve was all unbound,
And they express'd their rapture with their might,
In clamors meet to plague the soul of night.
By this, was every sluice of social glee
Set open wide, and fill'd and flooded quite ;
The noisy toast was Isabel, and she
The heroine of half an hour's celebrity.

XXV.

Now was the turn of careless Jeremiah,
Born to no household ; to no calling bred ;
Who ate, drank, joked, laugh'd, sung, and strumm'd
　　the lyre,
But knew no useful art to gain his bread,
Or rightful hold a place to lay his head.
A busy brain and high, convivial zeal
The patrimony he inherited ;
He could the social glow inspire and feel,
And genial Humor set on him her broadest seal.

XXVI.

Had Fate with friendly grace allow'd, he might
Have sat, with wits of high degree and name,
At tables of the rich, great parasite,
And stood with Brummel on the hill of fame.
Then had he touch'd his just ambition's aim,
With quaint conceits amused the world polite,
The toast of polish'd lord and lovely dame,
Nor toil'd nor spun, but shone in raiment bright,
And freely fed on costly dainties, unrequite.

XXVII.

But envious stars that grudg'd the gifts they gave
Those lib'ral gifts a meaner sphere assign'd,
Doom'd him to serve coarse churl and low-born knave,
And earn the potluck of the unrefined;
And Fortune, as illib'ral and unkind,
Her cold, capricious succor still denied.
Yet his strong spirit chafed not nor repined,
But Fate and stars and Fortune all defied
With indolent disdain and philosophic pride.

XXVIII.

He'd mock the sober airs of Sentiment,
Fantastic paint the serious face of Care,
And turn to unremorseful merriment
Such griefs as feeling hearts forever share.
Perhaps to tickle Sorrow he would dare,
Till she might giggle through her falling tears,
And prim, sedate Propriety ensnare
In toils of laughter. Now his voice he clears,
And thus beguiles the royst'ring rhymers' ready ears.

The Outcast.

A BALLAD.

Tell me, thou youth so pale and wan,
    And, prithee, tell me true,
What sorrow triumphs in thy soul?
    What woful chance dost rue?

Despair broods o'er thy countenance
    And sits within thine eyes,
And languidly thy gait and mien
    Echo thy melting sighs.

Has Death, with unrelenting step,
    Across thy threshold trod,
And carried ruthlessly away
    Some precious household god?

Or did more cruel Love invade
    Thy jocund, peaceful life,
And prick thee, for his wanton sport,
    To hopeless, inward strife?

Perhaps 't was Fortune builded frail
　　A structure fair and tall,
And placed thee on the giddy height
　　To crush thee with the fall.

Keep not thy grief all pent within,
　　But pour it in my ear ;
And I to bear the dismal load
　　Will help thee while I hear.

Now, was it flame, or was it flood,
　　Or was it fell disease ;
Or sword, or accident, or wrong
　　Consum'd thy spirit's ease ?

Thou look'st so sad and woe-begone,
　　My pity yearns to thee ;
May be the telling of thy tale
　　Can soothe thy misery.

Tell me, thou youth so pale and wan,
　　And, prithee, tell me true,
What sorrow triumphs in thy soul ?
　　What woful chance dost rue ?

4

Then listen, while I sadly do
    Pour out my doleful tale:
My father's village mansion stood
    Within a verdant vale,

My father's village mansion, where
    My childhood was caress'd;
Oh! were its shelter o'er me still,
    I even now were blest.

But swiftly flash'd the blissful years,
    Chasing each other by,
And took me from my mother to
    The university.

I studied long, I studied deep,
    And many books I read
In many tongues, till I at last
    Return'd a wight learnéd.

By this, it was full time, they said,
    That I the world should see:
So, gay with expectation, I
    Came to the great citie.

Here Fashion's daughters soon began
    My company to woo,

And pleas'd I rov̥ed in Splendor Street
   And Tinsel Avenue.

A dame did charm above the rest;
   She was of noble form;
Of beauteous features, comely grace,
   And manners kind and warm.

And she did charm me not the less,
   But rather more instead,
That she so gracefully half mourn'd
   A husband buriéd.

So sweetly she my love besought,
   I could not say her nay,
But bade her take all I could give:
   That was my happiest day.

But its dear raptures quickly went
   And left a cureless smart;
For artful was the widow's love,
   And guileful was her art.

She told me, with much fond caress,
   I should her bridegroom be;
She overcame my foolish heart
   And my innocencie.

A time she revel'd in the wealth
  Of all she so had won,
But soon forgot the vow to wed,
  And left me all undone.

And now I wander, in despair,
  Adown and up Broadway,
Where all the pure and happy throng
  " The Fallen ! " seem to say.

There is in all the earth no peace
  Nor hiding-place for me :
Why should the shame that with me bides
  Leave my despoiler free ?

She laughs in cruel triumph now,
  And all the while, they say,
She is the gladdest of the glad,
  The gayest of the gay.

And, ah ! the world on her will smile,
  In praise of her high charms ;
While I, in bitterness forlorn,
  Bewail my hapless harms !

XXIX.

A radiant smile on every list'ner's face,
Grown with the progress of the plaintive lay,
Wax'd audible, and, at the close, gave place
To many a boisterous and sincere huzza !
A storm the author's blushes failed to stay.
Each line each man would sep'rately admire,
And Laughter kept o'er all obstrep'rous sway,
Till Time at last impatient did require
The bow of the next bard in order, Obadiah.

XXX.

He was a scrivener, that all day long
With skillful pen o'er dreary parchment bent,
A grim attorney's ghastly group among,
Who to their daily toil like oxen went,
Nor stopp'd to think what their performance meant.
Unlike his fellows, he caught curious views
Of things behind each opaque document,
At night coquetted once with a coy muse
And writ what now the tender critic may peruse.

The Mortgage.

A SONNET.

The house is high, and decorated round
   With Architecture's cunningest inventions ;
   Within, Arts hold harmonious contentions,
And Luxury a temple there has found.
But o'er the roof and all the ample ground,
   Noiseless, yet of the most malign intentions,
   A viewless thing the master never mentions,
Though unto his sole vision it is bound,
Whether he wakes or sleeps, has settled firm,
   Henceforth to hang unbidden ever nigh,
Haunt all his hours close as th' undying worm,
   And, when he feeds his guests, unceasingly
Before him stalk, unseen of others' eyes,
Threat'ning to drive him from his paradise.

XXXI.

The list'ning rhymers chimed a vacant cough ;
The strain was well they all politely swore ;
Twere better still if cut less briefly off
And lengthen'd to a hundred verses more :
The theme were worthy to be essay'd o'er.
But quick forgot they, in a bumper long,
The brevity of Obed to deplore ;
And then, with call unanimous and strong,
Loud hail'd the youngest minstrel and his latest song.

XXXII.

A youth he was of one and twenty years,
A beard of silken down, and slender frame,
But lusty spirit, ignorant of tears,
And natural as the mountains whence he came,
Where lived his parents known to rural fame,
The one for honest wisdom, and the other
For virtues womanly of every name,
A pious and incomparable mother,
Whose influence in his breast the world could never
smother.

XXXIII.

Their prayers pursued their only child from home,
First while he linger'd yet at Learning's shrine,
Next cross'd the sea, adventurous to roam
Where every sight was strange to his young eyne,
Then sought the town, with law to store his mind.
Here fav'rite grew among, yet oft would leave
The fops of Fashion and her virgins fine,
For such society as to conceive
Had haply made those parents' pious souls to grieve.

XXXIV.

Still not perverse nor wicked was his heart,
Nor felt he scorn of virtue's decent ways;
Though sooth he seem'd to shun their sober part
Who give their youth to pray'r and godly praise,
And trudge the path of wisdom all their days.
But glow of youthful curiosity
Prick'd him to search what varying phase
He might behold of our humanity,
And every shape and shade of life he long'd to see.

XXXV.

With open eye and ear inquisitive,
Amused he saunter'd, sometimes long by night,
To find how they might think or act or live,
The hypocrites of Pleasure, who despite
And mock her name in many a hollow rite;
Feign mirth their wither'd souls can never share;
Still play, with painful toil, unfelt delight;
And holy Shame with brass defiance dare;
Poor, ghastly, chainéd prisoners of grim Despair.

XXXVI.

Nor to their temples that in splendor shine,
And bow'rs luxurious, alone would he
His perilous, Circean walk confine:
But roved in gay, unscar'd security,
With vulgar sinners and of low degree,
Amongst their meaner haunts and cheaper caves,
Where Vice, made uglier far by poverty,
In hideous, nightly orgies coarsely raves;
And Virtue dead, unconscious, Christian pity craves.

XXXVII.

From syrens such as these, with wise control,
He went unscathed; for their polluted air
Had no contagion for his healthy soul,
No spell their arts to bind his head's least hair.
What other scenes and characters would share
His busy leisure when his task was done,
I need not say, but legions strange they were,
And when the polished world for them he'd shun,
His honest brow and manners brave good welcome won.

XXXVIII.

He was the darling of this coterie;
And him their common voice dubb'd Princely Paul;
His every jest provoked their easy glee,
Their swift assent his grave opinions all;
But chief his muse their praises forth did call,
So full and fast, so frolicksome and free.
Yet, lest his name at bar might harm befall,
She was his secret, doom'd unknown to be,
Save to one group that oft her pranks (like this) would see.

Eveline:

A TALE.

IN THREE CANTOS.

My verse you may condemn, my theme you must admire.—CRABBE.

CANTO THE FIRST.

I.

Of love's unbridled chase the woes,
Of griefs that rage revengeful knows,
   From each the direful ills that spring,
And lack of favor Heaven shows
   Offending man and maid, I sing.

II.

In Cross street's mellow, placid shade,
   But few the years of grace agone,
   A nymph there dwelt, apast the dawn
Of charms that, when not marr'd, must fade.

The nymph was fair and froward too,
And many pleasing arts she knew,
But ah! a fearful sight to see
In any rage or jealousie;
For she was shapely not alone,
   Nor grace was all her motion's aim,
But strength in every limb it shone
   And vigor sat upon her frame;
While fury slumber'd in her eye
Or came forth in a tempest high.
Though Nature thus the nymph had blest,
The nymph did not in Nature rest,
But courted Science for a skill
Which humbled many at her will.
So panoplied, she sent forth Fear
To tease her foes both far and near;
And bore right merry sway and rough
O'er weaker, gentler human stuff;
Her very name inspired dread
As wide as e'er her fame had spread,
And many a nymph and many a swain,
In gore and sorrow, low had lain,
Sore trophies of the ruthless spleen
Or direful wrath of Eveline.

III.

Bill Pauling was an ocean knight,
A jolly, brawny, lusty wight;
And he was careless, bold, and free
As human craft right well could be;
And he had seen all far countrees,
A-coursing o'er storm-shaken seas;
On coasts of polar ice had run,
And stroll'd o'er isles beneath the sun;
But never yet, in either zone,
'Mong all Eve's daughters he had known,
Had Love's barb found his being's core,
Till, landed on Manhattan's shore,
While o'er the pave his footsteps stray'd,
By twilight's gently growing shade,
From worship fresh at Bacchus' shrine;
He overhaul'd the nymph divine,
Chaste Eveline, rigg'd daintily,
Whom to adore was but to see.

IV.

She said, " My dear, my only love,
Sweet darling, precious turtle dove!
O'er earth and sea where roamedst thou,
And hidst thyself from me till now?
5

Ah! wretched me! I've wander'd here
This dismal, long, unhappy year,
Still seeking whom I could adore,
But ne'er his image saw before.
Hope led me daily forth, to show
The depth of disappointment's woe;
While something told my heart 'twas vain,
For he, my fond, ideal swain,
And soul's sweet idol, roam'd the main.
But God be prais'd, in whose best time,
From his great goodness,—fount sublime,—
Each blessing and all mercies flow
To mortal creatures frail, below.
For He at last thy errant form.
Hath brought, through peril and through storm,
I pray not soon again to roam,
But long to rest in this heart's home.
Oh turn, sweet youth of gentle mien
Unto the bower of Eveline;
And, as we both do thither hie,
Some tropic fruits thy gold shall buy."

V.

She paus'd and, downward gazing, sigh'd,
While thus the melting swain replied :
" Fair Eveline, no rapture true
This torpid breast before e'er knew;

For, though each coast and clime hath shown
Me what of beauty was its own,
My soul, still trench'd in stubborn might,
Defied Love's weakness and delight,
And ne'er, until this blesséd hour,
I felt his soft, dissolving pow'r
Steal o'er each unresisting sense,
Resistless as omnipotence.
But here and now confess I must,
How vain hath been this heart's proud trust ;
This heart, once bold and stout, I ween,
Is at thy feet, oh ! Eveline.
That matchless mould, that peerless grace,
  ·The spirit radiant from those eyes,
  . And something still that underlies
The whole, their soft, effaceless trace,
Have sunk where nought could sink before,
To dwell thereon forevermore.
A void was in the soul of Bill
Which nought could e'er, but thou dost, fill.
What remnant drear of life were left
If 't were henceforth of thee bereft !
A gloom were all the future then,
More dark than ev'n the past has been.
Ah ! Memory holds no joys for me,
And, Hope, my refuge is to thee.
The present is the hour of bliss ;

Could all the future be like this,
Fore'er the gentle Eveline
I'd constant woo and constant win,
My heart's each thought were then supplied,
Nor its most vaulting wish denied ;
The hours should teem with joys divine,
Heav'n's own beatitude were mine,
Each transport should the last pursue
And dying raptures bring forth new."

VI.

Swift she with honied speech replied,
    And tones whose sweetness music made ;
And speaking eyes well told beside
    Whate'er her words might leave unsaid.
The easy knight of the blue wave,
    While converse and the moments sped,
Heard but the lady of the pave
    And follow'd where that syren led.

VII.

Erebus thick his shadows flung
    O'er Gotham's every mart and place ;
Anon the watchman's club-note rung
    Where darkness hid his silent pace.

Soft Dalliance then held Neptune's child
In unaccustom'd arms beguiled,
And fill'd with luring tales his ear,
Till orient, bright Aurora clear,
'Dawn's rosy-finger'd daughter's' beams
Dissolv'd the darkness and his dreams.

VIII.

What firm enchantment love doth weave,
  To wrap each faculty and sense
  In one brief ecstacy intense,
And then the cheated mortal leave!
Seductive power! yet fierce and fell,
That promis'st heav'n but givest hell,
They that have found, or yet shall find,
  But passing bliss and coming woe
  Gifts thine peculiar to bestow,
Have been, and still must be, mankind.
Who ever on thy transports drew,
Nor did the soft transaction rue?
Not youthful nymphs and swains alone
Thy sore experience have known;
But sages, statesmen, rakes and boys,
  With trulls and widows, maids and wives,
Have tasted thy grief-bringing joys
  To prove a poison of their lives.

IX.

And Fate had said that Bill that night
Should pass the ardent frenzy's height;
Should clutch at glories false as sand,
And find repentance in his hand.
Nature had piled the fuel high,
And wet wine wrought combustion dry;
When now at length Occasion came
And torch'd the easy-kindled flame.
At first, a gentle blaze it glow'd,
As through his veins it smoothly rode;
But soon, alas! impetuous grown,
The new-born ardor flash'd and shone,
And lick'd the air with demon tongue,
And fierce a song of fury sung.
Then Prudence fled her long-kept home,
And Passion revel'd through the dome;
Then Wisdom left a wonted throne,
And Folly ruled supreme alone.
Ah! hour of evil fate to Bill!
For, in its evanescent thrill,
He gave the charmer of his will
A pledge that he might not fulfill.

X.

As some gay meteor's treach'rous ray,
Athwart the evening traveler's way,
Decoys his sober feet astray
　　Where mire and blackness dread surround :
So passion holds to human sight
Of flitting joys a lurid light,
That tempts a moment's basking bright,
　　Then flashes out in night profound.

CANTO THE SECOND.

I.

Most classic shade of Orange street,
Where reigns the mind of Ebon Pete,
And motley pilgrims nightly greet
Her of the ' many-twinkling feet ' !
To thy most sanctified recess
At midnight came the votive press
Of worshipers from every race
That oft thy dusky precincts grace,
Europa's, Ethiop's, India's sons ;
Pale faces, sables, drabs and duns ;
And Frailty's daughters thickly came ;
Nobody's children, wild and tame ;
The reckless brood of easy Mirth,

And they whom Chance or Sin gave birth;
A heterogeneous company,
To honor great Terpsichore;
All blithe of limb and gay of mood;
And in the midst Bill Pauling stood.

II.

The violin, shrill shrieking, spoke
What first the temple's stillness broke;
The clattering castanet chimed in,
And join'd the thumping tambourine.
The prelude's echo domeward rung
To silence, when all wildly sung,—

The Song of the Shiftless.

1.

Life is foaming! take it now,
Nor insipid let it grow;
While it rises, tip it fast;
For its sparkling cannot last.

2.

Life's not substance, but is shade;
All its brightness glares to fade;
'Tis not tragic, but burlesque;
'Tis not earnest, but a jest.

3.

Melancholy is a fool;
Thought is Folly's solemn tool;
Duty-heeders are a race
Thrallèd under weakness base.

4.

Sober action is unblest;
So is holy sabbath rest;
Honor is of fiction wrought,
And condition is but nought.

5.

Round's the face of mother Earth,
Therefore should we honor Mirth;
Wisdom weeps not o'er life's jest,
But enjoys it with a zest.

6.

Life is foaming! take it now,
Nor insipid let it grow;
While it rises, tip it fast;
For its sparkling cannot last.

The scented breezes deftly bore
The careless, quick-forgotten strain
To staid Oblivion's darken'd door;
Who eager stands to entertain
Unnumber'd such with endless, free,
Devouring hospitality.

III.

Then rose the music's quicken'd swell,
And wrought a Terpsichorean spell ;
From porch to shrine the temple's ground
The stirring, light enchantment bound ;
And all the votaries, to and fro,
Tripp'd ' on the light fantastic toe ;'
In measur'd grace and courtly ways
They form'd and then dissolv'd each maze ;
They pass'd and whirl'd in motion free,
   Approach'd, receded, balanc'd, swung,
And on the heel of Harmony
   Each will and every spirit hung.

IV.

The portal hing'd to Eveline ;
Her eyes shot indignation keen ;
Straight on the sea-bred swain she bore,
   (Unconscious if earth had a woe
   He mov'd, but doom'd full soon to know
And taste the sorrows of the shore)
And thus, its fury ill supprest,
The anger in her soul confess'd :
" Presumptuous youth! to deem so light
What nature made our sex's right,

Ordain'd forever yours to bind,
And still confess'd by all mankind,—
The gallant duty none gainsay,
And most are ever proud to pay!
I here protest this debt to me
Long due, is still unpaid by thee.
Strange vanity thy soul possess'd,
 And insolence grown mad was thine,
To trust my rising ire should rest
 Till unto me thou render mine.
Thy soul some gay delusion fed
 With dreams that Mercy's care benign,
And mild Impunity, thy head
 Would shield through monstrous sin as thine.
The vow that unredeem'd I mourn
 Seem'd made by love that knows not death,
And to my ears was softly borne
 On Eloquence's ardent breath.
But ah! those gentle words beneath,
 Behind that language of the eyes,
Hid false tongue and malignant teeth;
 Deceit had stole such fair disguise.
In that blest hour, oh, falsely blest!
My fancy's vision saw me drest
In dazzling tint and texture fine,
The robe thou swore which should be mine.

Think not, vain type of man! thy oath
  Its deep force nimbly thus undone;
  Nor deem thy power or skill can shun
Its penalty and duty both.
Thy perjur'd heart let fear advise
What danger menaces thine eyes,
Till Eveline's shall fondly view
That plighted gown of dazzling hue."

V.

She paus'd while speech he meek essay'd :
" Thy sex's paragon, sweet maid,
That Power whose voice, though still and small,
Responds, whene'er we rightly call,
With counsels man must own divine,—
Whose heeded words and hints benign
Avert the complicated woes
That otherwise we self-impose,—
With charity whose spirit dwells
Forever, and whose maxim tells
That wit is out while wine is in,
Teach thee to palliate my sin.
Or yet, if reason's candid strain
  Thy stern, relentless wrath ignore,
Let gentle pity not in vain
  The ear of sympathy implore.

That luckless pledge I gave insane ;
Gin's subtle charm was on my brain,
With silent force, subduing, deep,
That wisdom lull'd in fatal sleep,
And all my will and action lent
To folly's loose, impetuous bent.
To own such debt, and reckless spurn   .
The rede man should from prudence learn,
Were mad to rush against those laws
Whose breach consigns to ruin's jaws.
For, know that Fortune hath to me
Slight favor shown and grudgingly ;
And should I, in a moment tame,
Discharge thy importuning claim,
Then Plutus, grimly led by Fate,
With fiercest frown, in direst hate,
Would hurl my timbers high ashore
And shun me thence forevermore.
Dismiss the dream that doth cajole
Thy unsophisticated soul,
Nor hope in canvas gay to shine
At such dread sacrifice of mine."
6

VI.

Volcanic fires, within her breast
Sore-pent, th' offended nymph possess'd;
And smother'd vengeance, bursting nigh,
Deep murmur'd through her low reply.
"Bold words! ah! little ween'st how bold,
For youth of such a slender mould.
But evanescent be the spell
 Which soothes thy wits, and lends the while
 Its brazen smirk thy front of guile,
That soon shall rather mirror hell.
In vain seeks falsehood's softest breath
To melt the hardness of my wrath;
And worse than vain, thy labor'd scorn,—
By wrong begot, of folly born;
This breast to fierce resentment burns,
And gentle rage to fury turns.
To-morrow mend thy broken vow!
Or dream this night of griefs enow,
And wake o'erwhelm'd by suff'ring dread
Of sorrows gathering o'er thy head.
Heed friendly words or soon shalt rue
A foe's unpitying deeds.   Adieu!"
She strode out loftily, this said,
And on the street evanishéd.

CANTO THE THIRD.

I.

Departing day was hast'ning past,
And night's grim front came following fast;
Unnumber'd noisy wheels were dumb,
And hush'd was traffic's loudest hum;
While o'er the town cold rainclouds hung
And, as by pluvial Genii wrung,
  Their dismal currents pour'd :
Intent each dryest nook to lave,
The flood fast patter'd on the pave;
Uplifted skirts then sigh'd for home,
  And soaking wand'rers homeward hied,
  With rueful faces, whilst the tide,
From reeking roof and dripping dome,
  Through eaves and gutters roar'd.
Frail awnings, drench'd, frail shelter spread
Where pausing groups, e'er-changing, sped;
And hapless swains, and nymphs forlorn,
That late had mov'd in slipper'd pride,—
Alas! how fallen since the morn!—
  In wilted sadness, envious, eyed
    Th' umbrellaed, booted throng :

While Comfort, snug at home intrench'd,
   Complacent through front windows peer'd,
   And covertly and dryly jeer'd
The passing crowd, that dripping, drench'd,
   And shiv'ring, rush'd along.

II.

Where Anthony with Little Water blends,
And Cow Bay worldward reeking sends
Her many-color'd denizens,
   An ancient mart affords,
What long the vicinage there found,
Its best supplies, by peck or pound,
Of fruits, and all provisions sound,
   That graced its sumptuous boards.

III.

Here came the hero of the deep,
  His trim exteriors to save,
As scuds the barque in storm to keep
  Some shelt'ring haven's friendly wave.
And pleasing refuge found he here
From pelting damps, thick, chill and drear;
But refuge none, perversely wills
Unpitying Fate, from direr ills.

For on his wake a freighted craft,
  Of wrath and retribution full,
  With threat'ning prow and stalwart hull,
Malignly hurried near abaft.

IV.

Soon face to face they stood once more ;
And, fiercer now than e'en before,
Her frown, terrific glooming, sore
    Smote sudden on his fears ;
While tones that bore envenom'd weight,
Breathing of vengeance and of hate,
Dread prelude as of tragic fate,
    Met stunningly his ears :
" Thy doom delay, now, most false man,
My patient wrongs no longer can ;
Fierce burns the passion smother'd here,
And expiation's time is near.
Speak not for mercy nor for truce ;
Thy words have parted with their use.
The lip once mark'd by falsehood's stain,
Can never its lost power regain ;
The heart once hurt by treachery's blow,
Can ne'er its former trust bestow.
No act may soften now my hate ;
Thy penitence were ev'n too late."

Thus she, when through the fragrant air,
First being pois'd with skillful care,
A quick-seiz'd, fierce-hurl'd *pomme de terre*
    Purpled his dexter eye ;
And his unguarded visage caught
What swift succession after brought,—
A *rùta baga* wildly flung,
Whose force both flesh and spirit stung.
A crimson flood each nostril spill'd,
And, most unwonted and unwill'd,
With sudden drops his orbs were fill'd,
    And burst his lips a sigh.

V.

Then rush'd they each to other's arms,
With fell intents for direst harms ;
In conflict wild they madly closed,
With skill and strength and will opposed ;
When soon he found his furious hold
No fragile, soft frame did enfold ;
And well she felt her arms of might
Encircled then no carpet knight.
An instant makes the conflict fierce ;
Her tigress teeth his cheek's flesh pierce ;

When, by the sudden anguish stung,
He quick his burden tripp'd and flung.
Supinely on the floor she fell,
Yet brought her foe the crash to swell;
Nor kept he long the topmost place,
For by a mighty *coup de grace,*
She show'd the rafters to his face.
His desperate will and furious main
The shifting vantage turn'd again;
And then athwart the stainéd floor
They to and fro went o'er and o'er.
The gathering crowd, from all the Five
Points, where the unwash'd swarm and hive,
Gave anxious and respectful way,
With most commoding surge and sway,
And loudest shouts for fairest play.

VI.

The gaping ring gap'd open now,
As, arm'd and bent to quell a row,
Four sturdy knaves of valiant mien,
All star-bedizen'd, strode between.
Two seiz'd the nymph, two the seiz'd the swain,

And, sund'ring rude the clinging twain,
Thence grimly forth, sore-panting, led
Their sullen and reluctant tread.
Devoted pair !   By Fate's decree
Devoted each to misery !
Ah ! woe was in th' expression sore
His bruis'd and bleeding visage wore,
As, brooding on the ill-starr'd day,
    With fancies of a donjon keep,
    Where soon should be his troubled sleep,
He silent took his guarded way.

VII.

Nor less was she unblest, for though
On one of her soft sex a blow
His gallant spirit scorn'd to bring,
He could inflict a sharper sting,—
Of sorrow an intenser shade ;
And much of that harsh pow'r he made.
For while, alas! she trusted well
Her wardrobe gay his might should swell,
Most dread reverse ! his rude hands tore
And pluck'd away ev'n what she wore.
Ah, nymph distress'd ! for, as she went,
Of robes despoil'd, of passion spent,

The curious gaze of followers coarse,
And gibes unkind from brawlers hoarse,
Smote on her vanquish'd spirit's pride,
    And crush'd its flow'r,—oh ! ruthless glee !—
    To feel that all expos'd should be
The charms and tears she could not hide.

VIII.

But wounds of flesh and hurts of soul,
Benignant time oft maketh whole ;
And wisdom's soothing, calm relief
Darts from the ashes of our grief.
So time and wisdom heal'd the pain
Of wayward nymph and careless swain ;
They thence two chasten'd spirits bloom'd :
Their bodies were that night entomb'd.

XXXIX.

Paul ceas'd. The tankards clink'd another chime,
The cheerful liquor swiftly flow'd again
From whose inverted mouths, the hundredth time,
To other mouths that upturn'd met it fain,
Like mouths of ducks that catch the falling rain.
Then out upon the sleepy air there rung,
Of jovial criticism, fresh peals amain ;
Mirth, like a ball, from each to each was flung,
And Wit danc'd genially on every wagging tongue.

XL.

By this, a rumble of the earliest cart
Abroad, the reign of silence to invade,
And lumb'ring loudly tow'rd the slumb'ring mart,
Their ears unready, unawares, dismay'd,
Proclaiming dawn's advent not long delay'd,—
Unwelcome signal for the scene to close.
Then all around their hurried farewells said,
When every rhyming guest reluctant rose
And, flitting ghost-like homeward, slunk to his repose.

XLI.

Oft-times they met.   Should any wish to know
What further varied numbers thence befel,
What fancies gleam'd from their discourse's flow,
What fine enjoyment crown'd their cheap revel;
The flatter'd Muse, loquacious, pleas'd would tell.
But never may she tune these notes again;
For household duty tasks her care too well,
Thrift bids her from the useless song refrain
And stern affairs dissever here the jolly strain.

THE END.